Praise for Goodnight Everyone:

"Genuinely magical ... this might just be every parent – and child's – dream book"

Huffington Post UK

"If this beautifully illustrated book doesn't persuade reluctant toddlers to settle down for a night's sleep then nothing will"

Irish Examiner

"I cannot wait to give it to every parent I know"

Irish Independent

"An infectious bedtime story, sure to prompt yawns in readers and their preschool listeners as well"

Kirkus Reviews

"The visual equivalent of a warm blanket, and an ideal bedtime read"

Irish Times

"A lulling bedtime story that will help little ones yawn along"

Booktrust

"A must for all collections"

School Library Journal, starred review

"Elevated by indented pages in hot pink and indigo tones, night-sky inspired characters, and a rather lovely star chart on the inside front cover"

Evening Standard

Shortlisted for the Irish Book Award
Nominated for the Kate Greenaway Medal

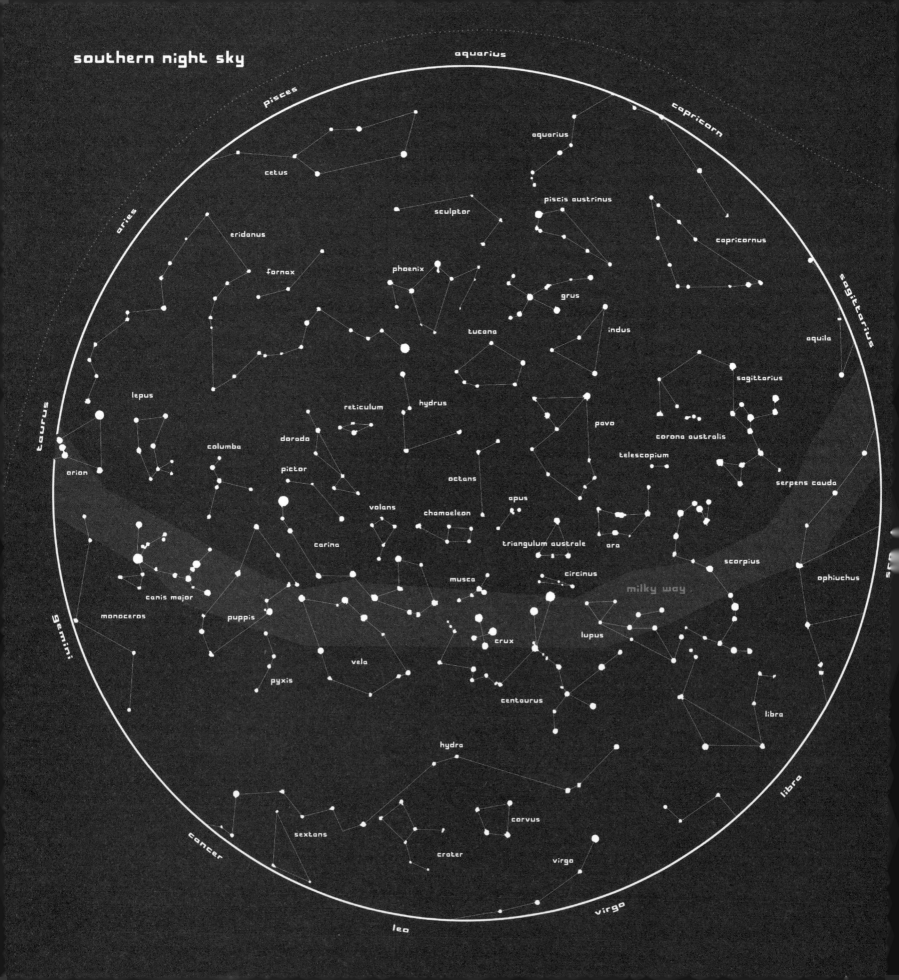

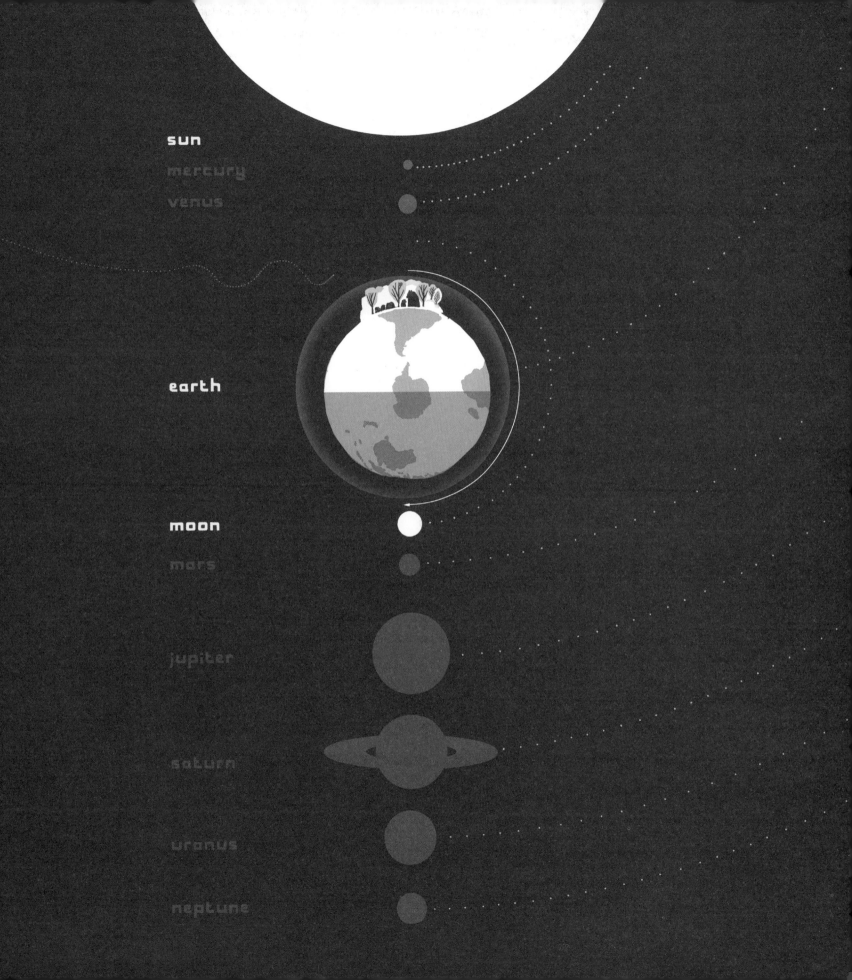

sun

mercury

venus

earth

moon

mars

jupiter

saturn

uranus

neptune

GOODNIGHT EVERYONE

"No dreamer is ever too small, no dream is ever too big."
anonymous

For my sister, Jan, a Montessori teacher,
who inspired the idea for this book

First published 2016 by Walker Books Ltd,
87 Vauxhall Walk, London SE11 5HJ

This edition published 2017

10 9 8 7 6 5 4 3 2 1

This book has been typeset in SHH

Printed in China

British Library Cataloguing in Publication Data:
a catalogue record for this book is
available from the British Library

ISBN 978-1-4063-7322-6

www.walker.co.uk

www.chrishaughton.com

WALKER BOOKS
AND SUBSIDIARIES

LONDON · BOSTON · SYDNEY · AUCKLAND

the sun is going down and everyone is sleepy

the mice

are sleepy

YAWN

the hares

are sleepy

they sigh

AH

the deer are sleepy

they take a long, deep breath

AHH..

even
Great
Big Bear
is sleepy

she has a
GREAT, BIG
STRETCH

AHHHH...............................

YAWN

"wanna play?" asks Little Bear

"we're too tired"

say the mice

"we're too

tired, too"

say the hares

"aren't you tired?" ask the deer

"oh no, no! not even a little bit"

says Little Bear

but after a
while, Little
Bear sighs

AH..................

takes a
long, deep
breath

AHHHH.........................

and has a

GREAT, BIG,

ENORMOUS

stretch

AHHHh........

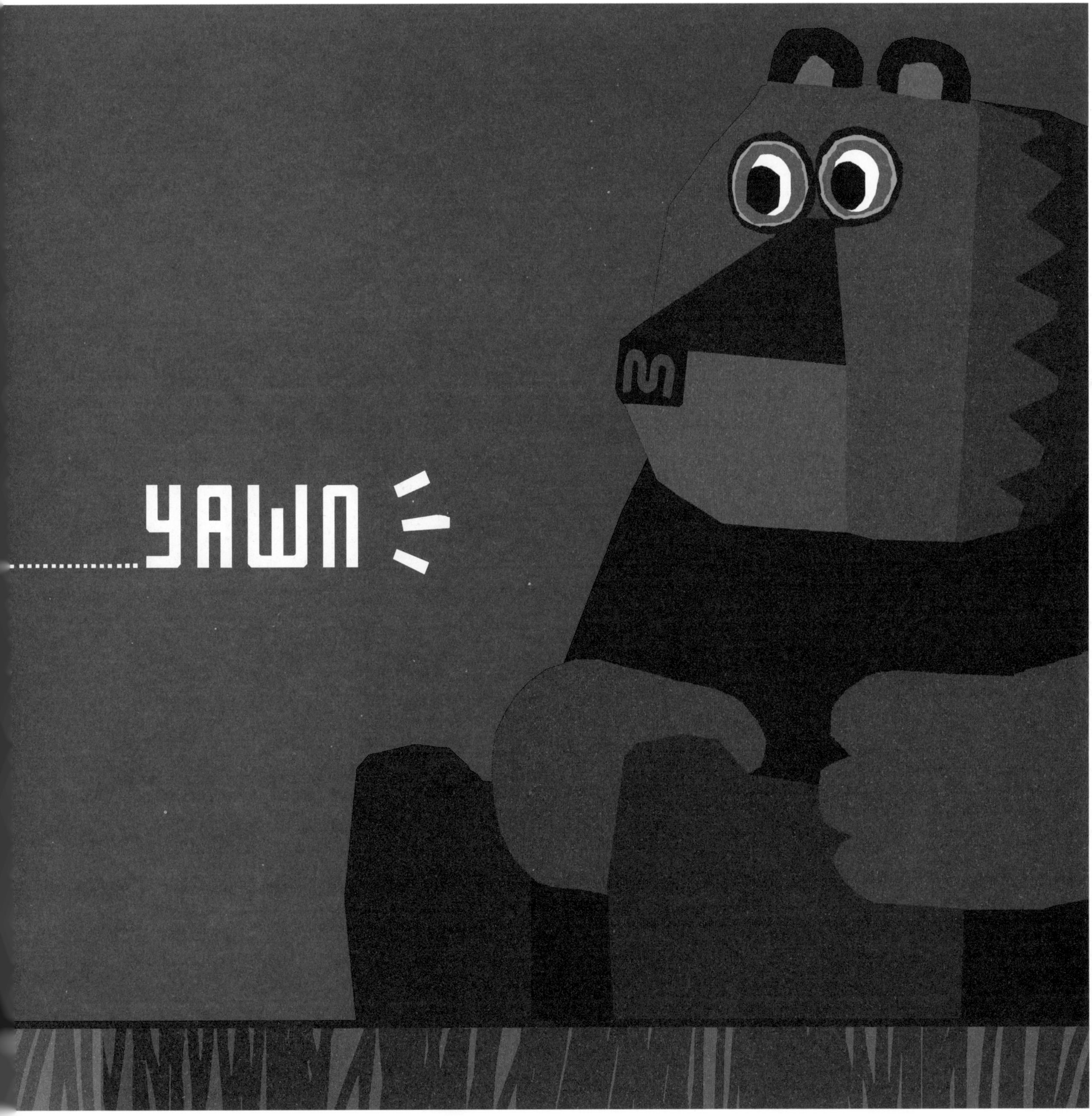
YAWN

"it really must
be time for bed"
says Great
Big Bear

the mice are asleep

they snore

. . . z z z

and sigh

S S S . . .

goodnight mice

the hares are asleep

. . . z z z Z Z Z

S S S s s s . . .

goodnight hares

the deer are asleep

...zzZZZZZZ

SSSSSSss...

goodnight deer

Little Bear

gets a great

big goodnight

kiss

∹ X ∺

goodnight bears

goodnight everyone

the moon is high and everyone is fast asleep

neptune

uranus

saturn

jupiter

mars

moon

earth

venus

mercury

sun

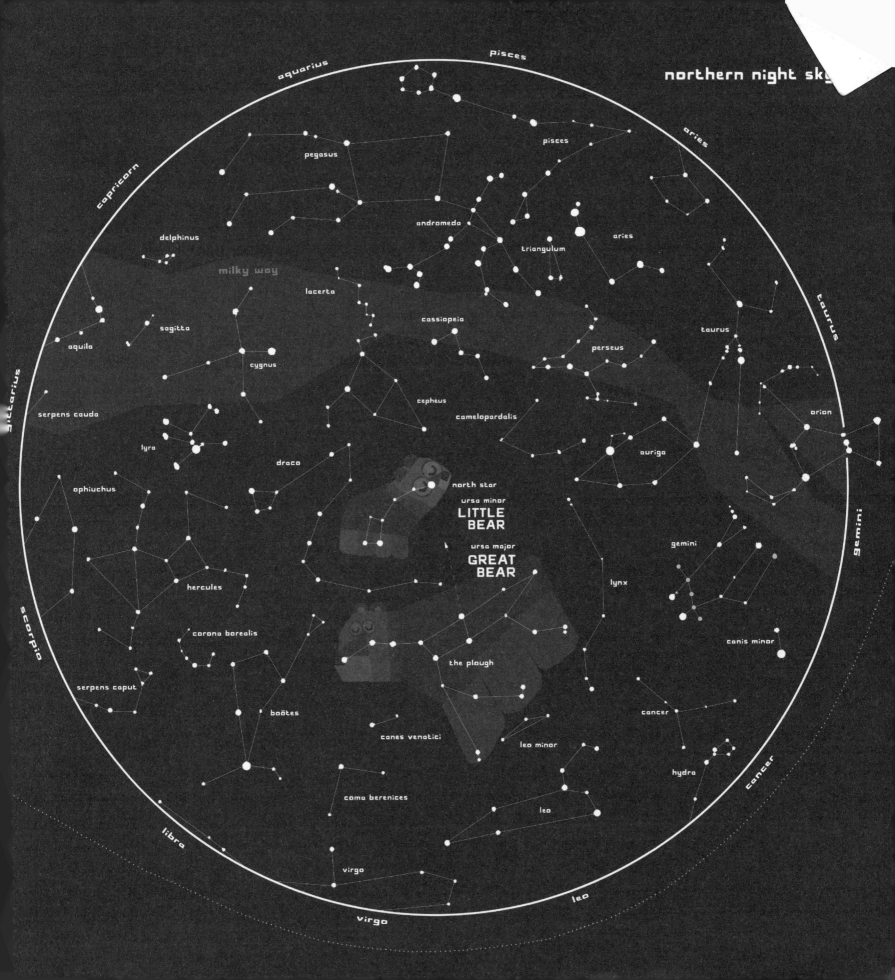

Look out for:

978-1-4063-3383-1   978-1-4063-4425-7

A BIT LOST

Winner of the Bisto Children's Book of the Year

Winner of a Booktrust Best New Illustrators Award

Winner of the Association of Illustrators
Children's Book Gold Award

978-1-4063-4476-9   978-1-4063-5791-2

OH NO, GEORGE!

Winner of the Junior Magazine
Picture Book of the Year

Shortlisted for the Roald Dahl Funny Prize

Shortlisted for the Kate Greenaway Medal

978-1-4063-6003-5   978-1-4063-6165-0

SHH! WE HAVE A PLAN

Winner of the Ezra Jack Keats New Illustrator Award

Winner of the Specsavers Irish Children's Book of the Year

Winner of the Association of Illustrators Award
for Children's Books

www.walker.co.uk

**Also by Chris Haughton:
Hat Monkey (app)**